PLEASE WASH YOUR HANDS BEFORE YOU READ ME AND KEEP ME CLEAN

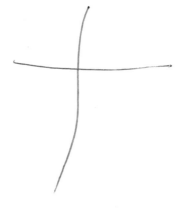

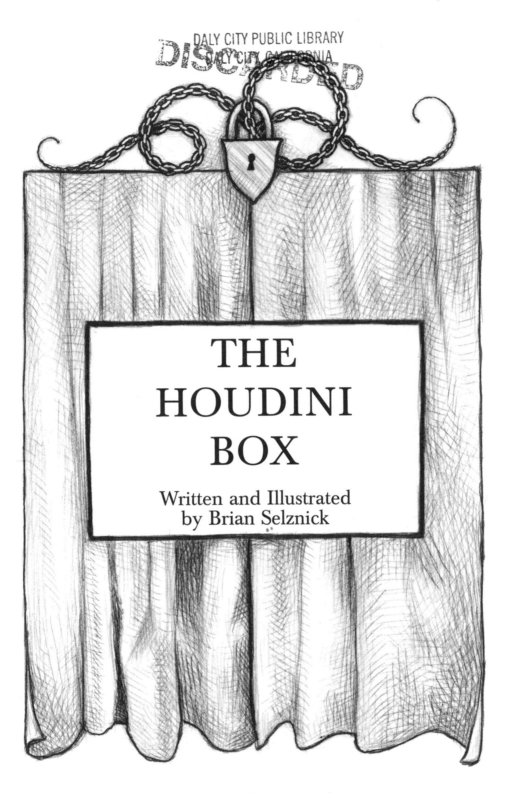

THE HOUDINI BOX

Written and Illustrated
by Brian Selznick

Aladdin Paperbacks
New York London Toronto Sydney Singapore

The poster "Harry Houdini: King of Cards" originally appeared in Milbourne
Christopher's *Houdini: A Pictorial Life* (New York, 1976) and is used here by the kind
permission of Mrs. Maurine Christopher.

First Aladdin Paperbacks edition September 2001
Copyright © 1991 by Brian Selznick

Aladdin Paperbacks
An imprint of Simon & Schuster
Children's Publishing Division
1230 Avenue of the Americas
New York, NY 10020

Also available in an Atheneum Books for Young Readers hardcover edition.

Book design by Mina Greenstein
Printed and bound in the United States of America
2 4 6 8 10 9 7 5 3 1

The Library of Congress has cataloged the original hardcover as follows:
Selznick, Brian
The Houdini box / by Brian Selznick
p.   cm.
Summary: A chance encounter with Harry Houdini leaves a
small boy in possession of a mysterious box—one that might
hold the secrets to the greatest magic tricks ever performed.
ISBN 0-679-81429-9 (original hc.)
[1. Magicians—Fiction. 2. Houdini, Harry, 1874-1926–
Fiction.] I. Title.   PZ7.S4654 Ho   1991   [Fic]—dc20
90-5387   CIP   AC
ISBN 0-698-84451-4 (Aladdin pbk.)

A
CURIOUS STORY
OF MAGIC
AND
ESCAPOLOGY
as performed by
Harry Houdini and a
little boy named Victor,
with special appearances
by Victor's Mother, Aunt
Harriet, and the lovely
Mrs. Houdini.

☞ We begin . . .

OUDINI was a magician. He could pull rabbits from hats, make elephants disappear, and do a thousand card tricks. Locks would fall open at his fingertips, and he could escape from ropes and chains and cabinets and coffins. Police from around the world couldn't keep him in their jails, and the oceans and the seas couldn't drown him. Bolt Houdini into a metal box and throw him in the water; he will escape. Lock him up in a jail, handcuffed and helpless, in any city in the world—Moscow, New York, Vienna, Paris, or Providence; Houdini will escape.

Everyone was wonderstruck by Houdini, but children were especially delighted. Children want to be able to escape from their rooms when they are sent there for being bad. They want to make their dinners disappear and their parents vanish. They want to pull candy from their pockets without putting any in, turn their sisters into puppies and their brothers into frogs (although some children want to turn their puppies and frogs into sisters and brothers). Children liked Houdini because he could do the unexplainable things that they wanted to do. Houdini was a magician. Magicians can do anything.

Victor was ten. He wanted to be a magician too.

When Victor was eight, he read in the newspaper that Houdini had escaped from an iron milk can in under twenty seconds.

Victor found his grandmother's trunk and closed himself inside. The locks snapped shut behind him. He tried and tried, but he could not escape in under twenty seconds. In fact, he could not escape at all.

So Victor cried and yelled until his mother came home and undid the locks. She was very upset that her son had shut himself up in Grandmother's trunk. Victor was very upset that he couldn't get out.

When Victor was nine, he found out that Houdini could hold his breath for over five thousand seconds while escaping from a crate dropped into the ocean. If Houdini could hold his breath for five thousand seconds in his crate in the ocean, then Victor could certainly hold his breath for five thousand seconds in his tub in the bathroom. So during bath time, he put his head underwater and counted as fast as he could. But he never got to five thousand. His mother kept making him get out of the tub and breathe.

Victor got this idea when he read that Houdini could walk through brick walls. Victor was sure he could do that. First he tried walking slowly into a living-room wall and pushing his way through. Nothing happened. Next he tried backing up across the room and running through the wall. He almost broke the lamp, the table, a few pictures, and his nose—but he didn't make it to the other side. Later that evening, after many unsuccessful hours, Victor finally got through the wall. He used the door.

Victor's mother was going crazy unlocking her son
from trunks, reminding him to breathe when he took
a bath, and telling him not to walk into walls. She
decided she would take him to visit Aunt Harriet.
Maybe a weekend in the country would calm him
down.

It was while they were traveling there that the most
incredible thing happened.

Victor was looking around the huge, bustling train station when he saw, way across the crowds, Harry Houdini himself, buying tickets with his wife.

Victor broke free from his mother's hand and ran straight to Houdini. He was filled with questions, millions and billions of questions, but which should he ask first? He took a deep breath, and this is what he said:

"How can I escape from my grandmother's trunk in under twenty seconds? How do I hold my breath in the tub without running out of air? Why can't I walk through a wall, like you can? How do you escape from jails and handcuffs and ropes and make elephants disappear? How—"

"Congratulations, my young man," interrupted the smiling magician. "No one has ever asked me so many questions in such a short amount of time. Are you a magician?"

"I want to be one," said Victor.

Houdini remained silent for several moments. After looking at Victor, and then at his wife, he finally said, "Then listen. Give me the tag from your suitcase."

"Why?"

"Your name and address are on it. When I write you a letter, I'll need to know where to send it, won't I?"

Victor immediately undid the little buckle and handed the tag to Houdini.

After reading it, the magician bent down so he was face to face with the boy. He whispered, "You want me to tell you things I can't talk about in the middle of a busy train station, son. And if I'm not mistaken, I see your mother heading this way. If it looks like you're going to get in trouble, you can blame everything on me." Then, grinning ever so slightly, he added, "Tell her Houdini tied you up for a moment. I'll write you a letter. Wait. Just you wait."

Houdini slipped the nametag into his pocket and disappeared into the crowd with his wife.

The weekend in the country was not as restful as Victor's mother had hoped. Her son was so excited about having seen Houdini that he locked himself in Aunt Harriet's dresser and in the cabinet of her clock. He walked very fast into her walls and almost broke all of her old framed photographs. Aunt Harriet was not sad when they left.

Back at home, Victor locked himself in the closet under the staircase, the cupboard in the kitchen, and his grandmother's trunk, nine more times. How he hoped Houdini would write him quickly!

Victor thought and dreamt about the magician's letter. When you are a boy expecting the secrets of the
world to arrive in the mail, it is almost impossible to
be patient. If only Victor were already a magician! A
magician could make the letter appear out of thin air.
But Victor was still just a boy, and patiently or not,
he had to wait. And so he did, until one day when he
was locked up tight inside an old suitcase, he finally
heard his mother say, "Victor, there's a letter here for
you."

She unlocked the suitcase and handed him the letter.
The handwriting was thick and round and perfect:

A thousand secrets await you.
Come to my house...

Then Houdini gave the time and date for the meeting.
But it seemed so far away! Victor knew he couldn't
wait so he went to the magician's house that evening.

His hands were shaking as he knocked on the door. With a heavy sigh it opened, and there before him was Harry Houdini's wife. Victor was suddenly too nervous to speak. He stood silently, staring at the sad woman in the light of the doorway.

She handed him some candy and softly asked, "What are you supposed to be?"

Victor didn't understand what she meant until he saw a ghost, a cowboy, and two little goblins running down the street. In all of his excitement, he had forgotten that tonight was Halloween!

And now he knew what he was supposed to be. "I'm a magician!" he said, and handed Mrs. Houdini the letter.

Mrs. Houdini read it and began to cry. She asked him to please wait inside, and vanished up the staircase into the magician's library, a dark place alive with books and dust and magical things. He held his breath, waiting for Houdini to greet him with outstretched arms and lead him back into that mysterious room.

When someone finally appeared in the hallway, though, it was only Mrs. Houdini again, alone. She came to Victor and handed him a small locked box. Then she opened the front door, and as she showed him out, he heard her whisper, "Houdini died today."

The magician's wife closed the door and left Victor alone with the box. "Bye," he said to the door, and went out, into the streets, toward home.

That night, while he was trying to open the lock on the box with pins and pens and all the small keys from the suitcases and clocks around the house, Victor found the owner's initials engraved on the bottom:

E. W.

This wasn't Houdini's box at all! The owner was some E. W. There could be no secrets in here.

Imagine, as you read this, how it would feel if you had one dream, one hope, one mysterious wish, and then saw it disappear into thin air. That's how Victor felt, and that's why he did what he did next. He took the box that belonged to E. W. and buried it forever at the bottom of his closet. As he closed the door, he made this promise: "Houdini is gone. I will never think about him again or try to do any of his tricks. Cross my heart and hope to die."

So VICTOR grew up and got married. He and his wife had a child, and they named him Harry (in honor of Aunt Harriet, who had passed away one October long ago; he was not named in honor of a certain magician, because Victor said he never, not even once, thought about Houdini).

One chilly day, several years later, Victor and Harry were playing ball in a large field near a graveyard behind their house. Victor was pitching and Harry was swinging his bat, but he could never quite hit the ball. It was nearing dark, and there was time for just one more try. Victor gave Harry a few last-minute batting tips, and then, with all the gentle power that he had, threw the day's final pitch to his son.

Harry closed his eyes, and at exactly the right moment, he swung his bat. He heard a loud crash, opened his eyes, and was amazed to see the ball fly through the sky and land somewhere in the middle of the graveyard.

Victor congratulated his son, and together they climbed over the iron fence to look for the winning baseball. At last they found it, lying in the corner of a dark monument. Whether it had landed there by chance, or by some strange, powerful magic, no one will ever know. But the ball that Victor's son had hit so perfectly had come to rest right on the grave of Houdini!

Victor read the monument. Two smaller words appeared directly below "Houdini," and Victor said them over and over again because they seemed so familiar. It wasn't until he traced the first letters with his fingers that he understood what he was reading. This was Houdini's real name.

Before he became Houdini, the magician had been a boy named Ehrich Weiss. E. W.!

Victor's head spun, and he laughed out loud. Carrying his son, he ran out of the graveyard, through the baseball field, and into his house.

He was out of breath and crazy with excitement, but he couldn't tell his wife or son what was going on. He waited until they were fast asleep, and then he snuck upstairs into the attic.

Victor found the forgotten box in a moonlit corner under a steady leak in the roof. He carefully picked it up and dried it off. His hand brushed across the lock, and it suddenly crumbled. The water had rusted through the tiny thing completely. How easy it would be to open the box now!

And that night, while his wife and son slept downstairs and the attic shadows vanished in the pale, blue fall of moonlight, Victor locked himself inside his grandmother's trunk and escaped

in under twenty seconds.

AN INTERESTING NOTE

The greatest magician of all time really was named Ehrich Weiss. But in reading the autobiography of Robert-Houdin, a haunting French magician, Ehrich found a hero and a new name. He added an *i* to the end of *Houdin*—thinking the name would then mean "like that person"—and the seventeen-year-old boy became *Houdini*.

Born on March 24, 1874, in Budapest, Hungary, Ehrich was the fifth son of a poor rabbi. The family came to the United States soon after Ehrich's birth, eventually settling in New York City. He was introduced to magic by a friend, and they practiced small conjuring tricks with cards and coins. But the secrets of rope escapes fascinated Ehrich the most.

With his new name, Houdini joined his brother in a small magic act until 1894, when he married Beatrice Rahner, a young show girl. Beatrice became his assistant, and they toured Europe in a show filled with magnificent escapes and mysteries. Audiences screamed and fainted and cheered. The Houdinis returned to America, triumphant.

When not performing, the magician wrote books, starred in fantastic movies, and visited famous magicians' graves. He was obsessed with death, and he and his wife promised that the first to die would try to contact the other.

Houdini really did die on Halloween, but it happened in Detroit while on tour, not in New York, as in my story. (I sent Houdini and his wife home so Victor could find them there that day.) Houdini was hospitalized on October 26, 1926, three days and four performances after being punched in the stomach by a college student wishing to test Houdini's incredible strength. As he lay dying, Houdini whispered "Rosabelle, believe" to his wife. After his death, this was the code she was to wait for. She never heard the words.

As for the Houdini box, I made it up—or at least I thought I did. I recently found a newspaper article, dated 1974, with the headline: "Magician's Box Still Being Sought." It went on to say: "[Houdini], who was born in 1874, reportedly said that on the 100th anniversary of the event, a box containing his cherished secrets would be made public. . . ." The article also said that the box had not yet been found.

—*Brian Selznick*

29

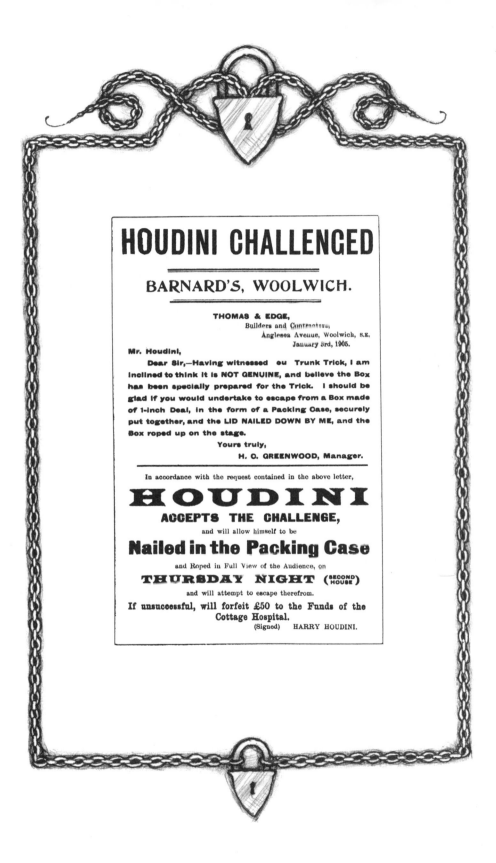

HOUDINI CHALLENGED

BARNARD'S, WOOLWICH.

THOMAS & EDGE,
Builders and Contractors,
Anglesea Avenue, Woolwich, S.E.
January 3rd, 1905.

Mr. Houdini,

Dear Sir,—Having witnessed eu Trunk Trick, I am inclined to think it is NOT GENUINE, and believe the Box has been specially prepared for the Trick. I should be glad if you would undertake to escape from a Box made of 1-inch Deal, in the form of a Packing Case, securely put together, and the LID NAILED DOWN BY ME, and the Box roped up on the stage.

Yours truly,

H. O. GREENWOOD, Manager.

In accordance with the request contained in the above letter,

HOUDINI

ACCEPTS THE CHALLENGE,

and will allow himself to be

Nailed in the Packing Case

and Roped in Full View of the Audience, on

THURSDAY NIGHT (SECOND HOUSE)

and will attempt to escape therefrom.

If unsuccessful, will forfeit £50 to the Funds of the Cottage Hospital.

(Signed)   HARRY HOUDINI.

1/4   10/63   1-3-04